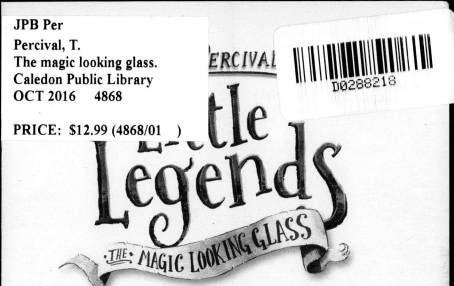

Tom Percival grew up in a remote and beautiful part of south Shropshire. It was so remote that he lived in a small caravan without mains electricity or any sensible form of heating. He thinks he's probably one of the few people in his peer group to have learned to read by gas lamp.

Having established a career as a picture-book author and illustrator, Little Legends is Tom's first chapter-book series for young readers. The idea for Little Legends was developed by Tom with Made in Me, a digital studio exploring new ways for technology and storytelling to inspire the next generation.

MACMILLAN CHILDREN'S BOOKS

This book is dedicated to Gastrells School and everyone in it, for being generally AWESOME!

First published 2016 by Macmillan Children's Books
an imprint of Pan Macmillan
20 New Wharf Road, London N1 9RR
Associated companies throughout the world
www.panmacmillan.com

ISBN 978-1-4472-9215-9

Contents

1

Trimming the Story Tree

It was the annual trimming of the Story Tree and *everyone* in Tale Town was excited. Even Sleeping Beauty was excited and she wasn't even awake, but she *looked* excited – sort of. The Story Tree was the reason that the town had first got its name – every one of its many leaves contained a different story. To 'read' them, all you had to do was run your finger along the leaf, and that story would happen *inside your head*.

With every new story that was told nearby, a new branch or shoot would sprout on the tree, so it could easily get very overgrown. This is why every year the oldest stories were trimmed from the tree, dried out, and turned into scrolls that were kept in a vault deep beneath the Tale Town library.

———◆◆◆———

Huge crowds had gathered to watch the ceremony, and Jack and Betsy, his magical talking hen, struggled to push their way to the front to meet their friends.

'Excuse me!' called out Jack as he elbowed his way

past three little pigs and three *much* larger bears. 'Coming through!'

'**PaaaAaArdon!**' squawked Betsy as she hopped up and down in front of Jack.

'Sorry?' said Jack. 'What was that, Betsy?'

Betsy rolled her eyes. The only word she'd ever been able to say was 'what', but somehow Jack always knew what she meant. Recently he'd been trying to teach her some more polite words, like 'pardon', but it wasn't really working out.

'**WHAaAaaaAaaat!**' shrieked Betsy crossly.

'Oh! I see . . .' said Jack. 'You're right, that *is* Sausage-Face Fitch, but you shouldn't call him that – Mayor Fitch would go crazy if he heard you! Come on, the ceremony's about to begin!'

⁘

'Hey, Jack –'

'– there you are!' said Hansel and Gretel as Jack finally got to the front of the crowd. The twins were close – *very* close. Sometimes they could have whole conversations just by waggling their eyebrows at each other.

'Hi, everyone!' called Jack, waving at his friends. Hansel, Gretel, Red and Anansi all waved back. 'Have I missed anything?' he added.

'Not really, but –'

'– Mayor Fitch is *still* –

'– doing his speech!' replied Hansel and Gretel.

The mayor was standing behind a podium, his shiny, pink face gleaming in the sunlight. He lifted up the ancient stone tablet that the poem 'Live Long the Story Tree' was carved into. *Everyone* in Tale Town knew the poem, which had been carved into the stone for almost as long as the town had been there:

Long ago, upon this spot the Story
    Tree was born,
And with it grew up Tale Town, a
    rose without a thorn.

Beware the shadows lurking in the
    darkness of the night,
Who want to take away this gift and
    hide from us its light.

For if this tree is damaged then
    expect the unexpected,
The Story Tree is sacred and must
    always be protected.

Live long the Story Tree!

Anansi scowled while two grumpy-looking spiders, perched on each of his shoulders, clacked their legs together crossly. Some people are afraid of spiders, but not Anansi: he *loved* them – and they loved him too.

'What is it, Anansi?' asked Jack, noticing his friend's stormy expression. 'I know we've all heard the poem a million times, but it's not *that* bad!'

'It's not the poem . . . it's *HIM*,' hissed Anansi, nodding towards Mayor Fitch. 'He *pretends* to be nice, but he can't be trusted! It's because of the trick he played on my Uncle Rufaro and his troll friend Hurrilan when they were children that my family are cursed to look like trolls!'

'I *still* can't believe that Rufaro was friends with a troll when he was young,' said Red. 'Especially now Hurrilan's the troll leader!'

'Back then Hurrilan was an outcast,' explained Anansi. 'He was living all alone in the woods and he saved Rufaro's life, remember?' His voice was lost in the roar of the crowd as everyone became *very* excited.

The Sacred Shiny Story-Snipping Shears had just been brought out by the mayor's guards. There was a spell of protection on the Story Tree, and the only way that *anything* could be cut from it was by using these magical shears. Mayor Fitch was holding them high above his head, preparing to make the first ceremonial snip, when a scream rose up through the crowd.

'*TROLLS!*' someone yelled. 'The trolls are coming!'

Immediately, Mayor Fitch's guards shot over to protect him, shoving the old lady who lived in a shoe into a muddy puddle. Jack and the others ran to help her as the rest of the crowd scattered.

———◆———

In all the confusion, the mayor had dropped the Sacred Shiny Story-Snipping Shears, and nobody but Jack seemed to have noticed. As his hand

reached out to pick up the
shears, he was barged out
of the way by a large, blue
creature with webbed
fingers and brightly
glowing eyes.

'I'll have those!'
said the creature,
smiling a thin
smile packed
full of needle-sharp
teeth. It waved its
hand and a torrent
of water
flooded over
Jack and Betsy,
sending them
skidding

backwards over the ground.

'WHAAAAT!?!' gurgled Betsy.

'It's a water troll!' cried Jack as he struggled to get to his feet in the muddy water. 'But how did it get past the Moonstone defences?'

Moonstone was the only thing that kept trolls out of Tale Town. The magical rocks weakened their magic and made them feel dizzy and sick – but *something* had obviously gone wrong.

Using the shears, the water troll hacked down the freshest, newest sprout from the Story Tree, then sprinted off – taking the shears and the cutting with him.

2

A Pale Imitation

Far away in the mountains, at the very edge of the trolls' land, smoke from a small, flickering fire rose up through a hole in the centre of a tent. Facing the fire was a large wooden throne covered in goatskins, upon which sprawled a tall, thin figure – a hooded cloak covering its face in darkness.

The entrance flap to the tent swung open and a broad, stocky earth troll bustled in.

'Hurrilan, sir,' he started, 'The troops are wondering –'

'Did I call for you?' interrupted the tall, thin figure.

'Er, well, no, but . . .'

'Then leave,' said Hurrilan. He moved one blue-green hand, making his fingers look as if they were turning around and walking away. The earth troll turned around and walked out with strange jerky movements, a look of horror on his face as he realized he was being controlled by Hurrilan's magic.

Moments later, a swirling light appeared in the middle of the tent and slowly formed into the shape of a man. He looked as though he was made of glass, almost completely see-through.

'You're late,' snapped Hurrilan.

'Sorry,' said the figure. 'You know how it is. Things always take longer than . . .' he trailed off. 'Still, I'm here now!' he added in a mumble.

'Will it work?' asked Hurrilan. 'Will the cutting from the Story Tree grow?'

'Definitely,' replied the figure. 'As long as your trolls can bring the cutting to me before sunset, I can make it grow.'

A smile crept across Hurrilan's face. 'Excellent!' he exclaimed. 'In that case, as soon as the cutting takes root and you find a suitable host . . . *you* will get what *you* want.'

The glass figure smiled greedily. 'Thank you!' he said, '*Thank you* for this—'

Hurrilan waved a hand and the transparent figure dissolved like a breaking wave. He leaned back slowly on his throne and smiled broadly. Soon the trolls would have their *own* Story Tree; soon *their* stories would be heard.

◆

As soon as it was discovered that the Sacred Shiny Story-Snipping Shears and a cutting from the Story Tree had been stolen, Mayor Fitch announced that everyone had to go home and stay in their houses. The Moonstone defences had been turned into mushrooms where the trolls came in, which meant that *someone* in Tale Town had allowed this to happen – someone with magic – and until the truth was discovered, *nobody* was allowed to do *anything*.

Rapunzel and her parents, the King and Queen, were away on an important royal engagement,* otherwise there was no way that the mayor would have got away with forcing everyone to stay at

---

* The important royal engagement was actually a royal camping holiday – although, as Rapunzel's mother was a *very* light sleeper, she had ordered some servants to take apart their private bedchambers and rebuild them on the campsite, including all their furniture *and* bathrooms, so it wasn't *really* camping.

home – especially as Rapunzel's father often called Mayor Fitch 'that horribly slimy man', even when they were in the same room.

Red, Anansi, Jack and Betsy were all being led back to their homes by a member of Mayor Fitch's guard.

'This is crazy!' whispered Jack. 'Nobody would let trolls in *on purpose*!'

'Perhaps . . .' replied Anansi, 'But if you ask me, Sausage-Face Fitch is enjoying all this a bit *too* much. You *know* how much he hates Rapunzel's parents – he wants to be completely in charge of Tale Town.'

'But we *all* saw the trolls take the cutting *and* the shears,' said Red, looking sideways at the guard to check he wasn't listening. 'Mayor Fitch certainly *looked* scared . . .'

'Well, *yeah*,' started Anansi. 'But that doesn't mean—'

'Silence!' barked the guard. 'We'll have less talk, and more walk! Do you think I've got nothing better to do?'

'**Whaaaaaat!**' said Betsy quietly, and Jack burst out laughing.

'*What?*' snapped the guard. 'What's so funny?'

'**Whaaaaaat...**' added Betsy, her eyes glinting mischievously.

'Someone tell me what that bird just said,' growled the guard, 'or I'm havin' chicken nuggets for lunch tomorrow!'

'She just said that you *do* look *very* busy,' said Jack, and the guard nodded self-importantly. '*Too busy to take a bath!*' Jack added in a whisper.

WHAAAA

Red and Anansi sniggered and then Anansi said in a hushed voice, 'Wait a minute . . . What happened to Hansel and Gretel?'

◆ ◆ ◆

Hansel and Gretel were walking through the woods outside Tale Town. As soon as the mayor's guards had started rounding people up, they had managed to slip silently away.

'What do you think is going on with Sausage-Face Fitch?' asked Hansel. 'Why would he put the whole town on lockdown?'

'I don't know,' replied Gretel. 'I guess he thinks someone's helping the trolls. How about we –'

'– follow the troll's tracks? See if we can find out what's going on?' finished Hansel. 'Good idea.' He pointed down to a roughly snapped branch and a large footprint on the forest floor.

'This is almost *too* easy!' said Gretel, then paused. 'Do you think we should tell Dad what we're doing?'

'I thought he was off on holiday with our new stepmum, Valerie?'

'Oh yeah! I forgot. I thought she

was called Susan, though?'

'No, Susan was last year,' corrected Hansel. 'Then there was Andrea, then Atsuko and *now* Valerie. She's *OK*, I guess . . . not as bossy as Susan – and nowhere *near* as mean as Atsuko.'

'She was the *worst*!' agreed Gretel. 'Always sending us off on those picnics in Bear Maul woods, and those swimming trips in Piranha Lagoon! Wasn't it weird that she always forgot to bring her *own* swimming things?'

They walked on in silence for a while, wondering who it was that decided that *all* stepmothers in the Fairytale Kingdom had to be awful – it was a *really* annoying law.

3

A Sheep in Wolf's Clothing

*T*he twins had been following the trolls' trail for almost half a day. They had stopped by a babbling brook to have something to eat, but the brook just kept *on* babbling. At first they'd listened politely – but it just wouldn't stop talking – so they'd crept silently away.

They were walking on through the woods when Gretel stopped abruptly

SNIFFFFFF!

and sniffed the air. '*Wolves!*' she hissed. 'I can smell them.' She stopped and sniffed again, then frowned, looking confused.

'I can smell something else too . . .' Hansel added. 'Is that –'

'– *fabric softener?*' said Gretel. They looked at each other, then crept through the bushes towards the scent.

In the middle of a small clearing sat a wolf. He was only young, little more than a cub, and he didn't look very scary – partly because his face looked so open and gentle, and his fur seemed so soft that it might have been blow-dried, but mainly because he was wearing a jaunty little cap and had a handkerchief tied around his neck.

'You can come out if you want,' said the wolf, 'I can hear you rustling about.'

'Oh . . . er –'

'– right . . . will do,' said Hansel and Gretel as they scrambled out of the bushes.

'Are you from Tale Town?' asked the wolf.

Hansel and Gretel looked at each other, having one of their silent, eyebrow-wiggling conversations as they tried to work out whether they could trust this wolf cub. Like trolls, wolves were *bad news* in Tale Town, but this young cub seemed different.

'Yes,' they said, eventually. 'We are.'

'Oh I would *love* to visit Tale Town!' said the wolf wistfully. 'Just imagine . . . The buzz! The cafes! The parties! But my dad won't have any of it. He's always like "*Wolves are wolves, son! We're not like them. We eat, we scheme, we steal, we go to the toilet OUTSIDE in the woods and we don't, on ANY account, use toilet paper*".' The young wolf wrinkled his nose. 'Seriously! He expects me to use *leaves* or something – it's totally gross!'

'You're not like any of the other wolves I've ever met,' said Hansel. 'You seem so much more . . .'

'Soft? Lame? Feeble? Un-terrifying? *Pathetic?*' asked the wolf. '*Yes*, I've heard it all before . . .'

'I was going to say *nice*, actually,' said Hansel. 'Anyway, I'm Hansel and this is Gretel.'

'I'm Wolfson, born of Greymist, grandson of Throat-Rip the Destroyer,' replied the wolf. 'But I prefer *Wolfie*. I've never liked having 'Throat-Rip' in my name. So *aggressive*!'

'I suppose so,' said Gretel with a smile.

'So, what are you doing out here?' asked Wolfie. 'You're

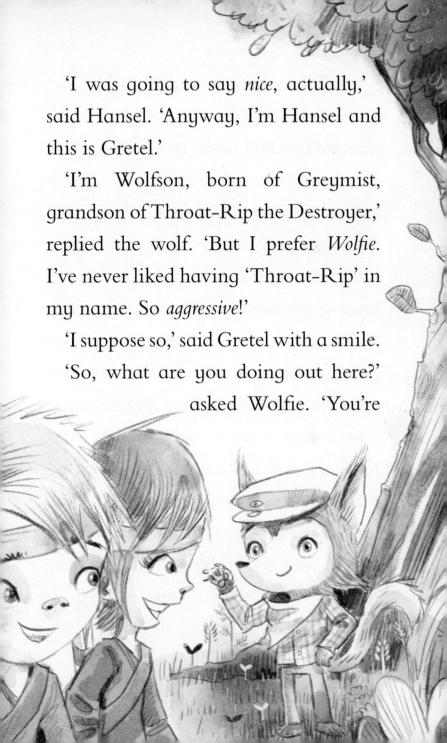

a long way from home.'

Hansel and Gretel told Wolfie all about what had happened back in Tale Town – how the trolls had stolen a cutting from the Story Tree along with the sacred shears, and how the mayor had put the whole town on lockdown until he got to the bottom of it all. They explained that they were going to try to get back the shears *and* the cutting.

Wolfie's eyes flashed with excitement. 'Oh, I would *love* to do something like that!' he said. 'Doing something *good*, for once! I'm always saying to Dad, "We should try to make friends in Tale Town, you know? Stop swallowing up grandmothers whole. People just don't like that sort of thing, it makes them feel sad. Why would you *want* to make people sad?"'

'I always thought it was –'

'– instinct or something?' said Hansel and Gretel.

'Well, *maybe*,' said Wolfie. 'But *no more*! I'm going to show Tale Town that not all wolves are bloodthirsty granny gobblers and pig-tricking cheats and liars! I'm going to come with you! I'm going to prove that wolves . . . can be *good*!' He paused, slightly out of breath after his speech. 'Er, that's as long as you guys don't mind if I tag along?'

The twins laughed. 'The more the merrier!' they said in unison.

'Do you need to get anything before we go?' asked Gretel.

'Actually, it's probably best that I don't go back home first,' replied Wolfie. 'Dad might ask questions and—'

'WOLFSON!' roared a deep, growling voice through the trees.

Wolfie's eyes shot wide open. 'It's Dad!' he whispered frantically. *'Hide!'*

'Who you talkin' to?' demanded the voice, getting closer now. 'I can smell *'umans*!'

Wolfie's eyes twitched this way and that as he tried to work out what to do. Then he had an idea. 'Run!' he whispered. *'As fast as you can!'*

'It's . . . er, humans all right, Dad!' he shouted back to his father. 'I'd been tracking them for ages and now you've scared them off!'

'Well, blow me! I'm sorry,' bellowed the huge, grizzled grey wolf as he burst into the clearing. 'I didn't realize. Still, we can catch 'em and tear them apart *together*.'

'Um, thanks, Dad,' said Wolfie. 'But this is something I really want to do *myself*. I'll, er . . . totally gut them and . . .' He paused uncertainly. 'Wear their toes as a necklace?'

'Good lad, Wolfson!' chuckled Wolfie's dad, or as most people called him, the Big Bad Wolf. 'I *always* knew you had it in yer!'

4

The Green Man's Lair

*H*ansel and Gretel always thought that they were the *best* at following trails, tracks, breadcrumbs, stones, or the delicious scent of gingerbread – but that was before they met Wolfie. He might not have enjoyed some of the more grisly things about being a wolf, but it *did* give him an amazing sense of smell and hearing. It wasn't long before they found themselves outside a huge wooden wall that grew right out of the ground.

'What is –'

'– this place?' marvelled Hansel and Gretel. Brambles were woven in and around the living wall; thorns the size of hands spiking dangerously outward.

'I've been here before,' said Wolfie thoughtfully. 'But it didn't look like this! The wall was much lower and there were lots of plants and flowers growing everywhere. A Green Man lived here, a kind of nature wizard. He loved *everything* about nature – even wolves! But now it feels so *unfriendly*.'

'And, this is where –'

'– the trail ends?' asked Hansel and Gretel.

'Afraid so,' said Wolfie, shivering a bit. 'So I guess we'd better go back and tell someone else? You know, like someone big, with weapons and an army and stuff?'

'Hmm, backup *would* be a good idea . . .' said Gretel. 'But it would take too long –'

'– and as we've come this far,' added Hansel, 'maybe we should just take a quick look inside?'

'Wow!' said Wolfie as he poked his head up over the top of the wall. 'Just, you know . . . *wow*!'

'What is it?' asked Hansel, who was climbing up behind him.

'It's *troll central* in there!' replied Wolfie. 'I don't think I've ever seen so many trolls, outside of a *Where's Trolly?* book!'

There were huge earth trolls with dull green skin and thick, muscular bodies, and blue water trolls with scales and webbed fingers and toes. There were even a few wind trolls, tall and thin, with long hair that billowed out, even when the air was perfectly still.

'What are they all doing here together?' asked Hansel. 'I thought the different troll clans didn't really mix.'

'No idea!' replied Gretel. 'But forget *that* – how are we going to find the cutting from the Story Tree?'

'Forget *that*!' said Wolfie. 'How are we even going to get *in*?'

———— ◆ ————

On the other side of the wall was a large courtyard filled with ferocious statues of wild animals. Trolls milled around, carrying crates of supplies and weapons or just sitting around playing cards. In the middle of the courtyard rose a huge, living palace. It was made in the same way as the wall they were perched on – trees and plants had knitted together and grown into towers, rooms, roofs and windows. The whole thing was covered with a tangled mass of dark, thorny brambles.

'We have to split up,' said Gretel. 'We'll get spotted for *sure* if we try to get in together, but if we go one-by-one we *should* be OK.'

Wolfie shuddered at the use of the word 'should'. 'How about I wait here?' he suggested. 'And keep lookout?'

'We'll cover more ground if we *all* go in,' said Gretel firmly.

'Mmm, right,' muttered Wolfie. 'Is there a secret signal for if we get into trouble?'

'How about we bleat like a goat?'

suggested Hansel.

'A *goat*?' asked Wolfie. 'Are you serious? Trolls *eat* goats – they'll come running!'

'Good point,' said Hansel. 'How about a raccoon?'

'What do *they* even sound like?' asked Gretel.

'An owl?' suggested Wolfie.

'It's the middle of the day!' protested Hansel and Gretel.

'All right,' said Wolfie sarcastically. 'How about we just yell, "*Help! I'm in trouble!*"?'

'Works for me,' replied Hansel. 'I

guess if things get *that* bad, then it won't really matter anyway!'

Hansel and Gretel looked bright-eyed and excited. Wolfie looked like he wanted to be sick.

———◆———

Hansel climbed silently down the thorn-covered wall. He moved like water, flowing from hiding place to hiding place. It was as though he knew *exactly* where each troll was, without even having to look. Within seconds he had dashed over to the wooden palace. He paused to give a quick thumbs-up to Gretel and Wolfie, before inching a door open and slipping inside.

'Whoa! How did he *do* that?' asked Wolfie. 'That was *amazing*!'

Gretel shrugged. 'When you spend enough time on your own you get good at looking after yourself! But you'd know all about that sort of thing, being a wolf, right?' She grinned at Wolfie as she scrambled down the wall, darting across the courtyard and taking cover behind a barrel. When there were no trolls looking she shot across to a pile of crates near a large locked door and managed to climb up to an open window without making a sound. She twisted in through the small opening and was lost from sight.

Wolfie sat on the top of the wall,

sweating with fear. He lowered one of his paws on to the branch below and had to clamp his mouth shut as he stepped on a big thorn. He was *probably* bleeding! Maybe he'd get rabies, or tetanus, or some other horrible infection . . .

After taking a few deep breaths, he carried on clumsily, hardly daring to look down and hoping with all his heart that if he couldn't see the trolls, then *they* couldn't see him. After what felt like forever, he finally had both feet safely on the ground. He cowered behind a big pile of ropes and wondered what he was going to do next. Just then a bell rang out and a voice bellowed, '*Dinner's ready!*'

All the trolls hurried off

into a small, leafy canteen building, chattering about what they hoped was going to be for dinner and, if there was going to be pudding, whether it would be goat ice cream – which they all seemed to agree was their favourite.

Wolfie watched one last hungry-looking troll lope into the canteen. Aside from the scary animal statues, the whole place was completely deserted. He smiled slightly as he crept out of his hiding place and scampered across the courtyard.

Hansel crept down a long, dark tunnel. He strained his ears for the sound of any approaching trolls, but could hear nothing. The corridor was uneven and plants and ferns grew everywhere, blocking his way. He tiptoed along, not knowing exactly what he was looking for, but hoping that he'd know it when he saw it.

What he *wasn't* expecting to find was Gretel. They both silently crept around a corner and came face to face with each other, eyes wide with surprise.

Hansel wiggled one eyebrow to mean: 'Have you seen any trolls?'

Gretel shifted her eyes to the left to

reply: 'No, I've not seen a single troll since I came in.'

Hansel wrinkled his nose to say: 'Me neither. Perhaps it's only the outside that's guarded?'

Gretel grinned and shrugged to say: 'Then why aren't we talking out loud?'

'No idea!' whispered Hansel. 'Come on, let's see what we can see!'

———◆◆———

Together they explored the living palace, looking in every room. Just as they were approaching the end of a corridor, there was a blue-grey blur as something disappeared around the corner.

'What was *that*?' asked Hansel.

'I've got no idea—' began Gretel.

'*Help!*' interrupted a nearby voice. 'Please, you *must* help me!'

Gretel shot a worried look at her brother.

'*Please . . .*' continued the voice desperately, 'you *have* to help me!'

Gretel raised an eyebrow to say: 'What should we do?'

Hansel narrowed his eyes, meaning: 'We'd better investigate!'

The twins peered into a room that was empty, apart from a large golden mirror. It had curling decorations all around the frame and a glassy surface that shifted and swirled with different colours. In the mirror was the reflection of a man – even though the room was empty.

'*Whoa!*' breathed Hansel. 'A magic looking glass!'

The figure in the mirror peered out with scared eyes. 'Oh, please say that you'll help,' it begged. '*Please!*'

'Why?' asked Gretel from the doorway. 'What's happened?'

'It's my master, the Green Man!' gasped the mirror. 'The trolls have

placed him under a spell and are using his powers to keep a cutting alive from a tree that can grow stories!'

'We know that the trolls took a cutting from the Story Tree,' gasped Hansel.

'We saw it happen!' added Gretel.

'I know where the cutting is being kept!' said the mirror. '*You* have to help me get the cutting away from here, so I can break the trolls' spell and free my master. Will you help?'

'If we *do* help –' began Gretel.

'– can we take the cutting back to Tale Town?' finished Hansel.

'Of course!' said the mirror. 'I just want my master back. So you'll help me?'

Hansel and Gretel looked at each other. '*Yes*,' they said. 'We will.'

'Marvellous!' exclaimed the mirror. 'Well, come in, *come in*!'

5

Body Snatcher

Hansel and Gretel stood at the edge of the room, looking at the magic mirror. The figure behind the glass smiled warmly at them. 'Sorry . . . could you both just come a bit closer please?' it asked. 'My eyesight's not what it used to be.'

'OK,' said Gretel as they walked into the room. 'So . . . where's the cutting?'

'Gosh! Aren't you *keen*!' exclaimed

the mirror. 'I must say, I simply couldn't do this without you! *Fnnnnrrp!*'

'Sorry, what was that?' asked Hansel.

'What was *what*?' replied the mirror.

'That sort of *snort*,' said Gretel.

'Like you were trying not to laugh?' added Hansel.

'Oh, *that*?' replied the mirror. 'No, no, no . . . it's just . . . I get hay fever at this time of year.'

'*Right* . . .' said Hansel, glancing over at Gretel suspiciously.

Suddenly the door swung shut behind them with a loud bang, and the mirror laughed a long and horrible laugh. '*Ha!*' exclaimed the mirror. '*Now* you are at my *mercy*!' The reflection paused and patted down all of its pockets. 'Now, where did I put my mercy? I'm *sure* I put it *somewhere*? Oh yes! *Now* I remember! I don't have any – I am mercy-less! *MERCILESS*!' It laughed again.

'Wow, that was the lamest joke *ever*!' whispered Hansel.

'Yeah!' agreed Gretel. 'Come on, *let's get out of here*!'

They turned to run out of the room, but their legs stiffened and slowed down, until they couldn't move at all.

Hansel gave Gretel a look that said: 'This isn't good!'

Gretel thought a message back to her

brother: '*Shall we use the secret signal?*'

Hansel nodded in agreement and then they both yelled as loud as they could:

'Help! We're in trouble!'

———◆———

Wolfie frowned as he padded down *another* empty corridor. It was as though the wooden palace was completely deserted. He'd seen no sign of the Green Man, or any trolls, but *that* was no bad thing. He wasn't entirely sure what his plan would be if he got spotted by a troll, but he thought it would probably involve quite a lot of running away, screaming '*AAAaaaaarrrrghhhh*'.

A distant sound made Wolfie's hair stand up on end. He could hear the signal for help echoing down the corridors.

'*Help! We're in trouble!*'

With barely a thought to his safety – apart from the obvious things, like how he *really* didn't want to get trapped, or hurt, or kidnapped, or eaten, or squashed, or bruised, or anything horrible like that – Wolfie turned and ran to help his friends.

◆◆

Neither Hansel nor Gretel could move their legs at all. They stood there, frozen, as the door swung open and a few blue-grey imps scampered into the room and dragged the mirror round on a small wheeled trolley so that it was facing them again.

'Nice of you to *stick around*,' said the magic mirror.

'What do you want?' asked Hansel coldly.

'Well . . . *you*, I suppose,' replied the mirror. 'You see, I've always been rather held back by the whole "magic looking glass" thing. I mean, I can leave for a short while . . .'

Hansel and Gretel both gasped as the reflection stepped out of the mirror, right in front of them.

'But it's not *enough*!' complained the reflection, swiping its hand soundlessly through Hansel's chest, making him flinch although he felt nothing.

'I can't *actually* touch anything!' explained the reflection. 'I'm not *really* real! But with one of your bodies, and my troll friend's help? Well, then *I* can be real – and it will be *you* rotting away in this mirror instead!'

———◆———

Wolfie's breath came in gasps as he ran as fast as he could down the hallway, knocking over plant pots and breaking saplings that grew up from the floor in his hurry. From behind a half-open door ahead he could hear a voice he didn't recognize saying, 'All I have to do is summon the troll warlock, and then I will be free of this mirror – *forever*! I'll be able to dance outside in the rain, *feel* the wind on my face! I'll be able to actually *smell* flowers as I brush my hand against them *and* kick down small children's sandcastles – it's going to be *amazing*!'

Wolfie held his breath as he pressed himself flat against the wall and peered through the doorway. Hansel and Gretel looked very uncomfortable – their legs frozen in a running position.

'You'll *never* take my body!' yelled Hansel.

'Or mine!' spat Gretel.

'Oh but I *will!*' said the mirror. 'I can do whatever I like! Witness: I shall swap your personalities! As simply as . . . *THIS!*' The reflection laughed as it pointed at each twin and then crossed its hands over. A glow trailed from each hand, swirling around Hansel and Gretel's heads, and for a moment, both of their faces went limp.

The reflection clicked its fingers. 'There! You have had your personalities switched! Your minds are in the wrong bodies! I can only imagine the *horror*! The *fear* that you must feel right now! *Now* do you see? *Now* do you feel the *awful* depths of my power?'

6

Role Reversal

Wolfie looked around. He had to do *something* to help – but what? He didn't have any tools or weapons. It was *hopeless*! Then he spotted a wooden bucket of muddy water.

'I wonder . . .' he thought as he grabbed the bucket.

Inside the room, the reflection gazed expectantly at the twins, and then frowned.

'Whoa!' said Gretel from Hansel's body. 'This is kind of weird – I never realized that you don't like broccoli?'

'No, not really . . .' admitted Hansel from Gretel's body. 'It looks a bit too much like a tiny tree, you know what I mean? Anyway, I like how you have your hair a bit longer. It feels nice!'

'*No, no, no, NO!*' shrieked the mirror. 'This isn't right! You're meant to be paralysed with fear, begging for mercy!'

'Well, you already made that lame joke about not having any –' said Gretel.

'– so what's the point?' finished Hansel, 'Besides, *you* don't scare us! We've seen off worse creatures than you!'

'*Really?*' asked the reflection. 'Worse than me?'

'Yeah!' said Gretel, 'Together we can do *anything*!'

The reflection grinned.

'Well then, let's see how you like it when you can't do *anything* together!' The reflection pointed at the twins again, a glowing light snaking from its hands towards them. The light grew brighter until, with a brief, blinding flash, it fell away.

Hansel and Gretel were back in their own bodies and free to move again. But instead of looking happy, they looked furious.

'This is all *your* fault!' shouted Gretel at Hansel.

'No way!' hissed Hansel. 'It's *YOUR* fault! I don't know why I've put up with you for so long!'

The reflection smiled wickedly.

'I'm going to do something I should have done a long time ago!' muttered Gretel, taking a step towards Hansel waving her candy-cane staff in the air.

'Suits me!' said Hansel. 'It's *about time* somebody taught you some manners!'

He pulled his candy-cane nunchucks off his back and swirled them through the air.

The reflection gurgled with delight. 'So *now* do you feel my pow*arghhhhhh*!'

There was a loud muddy *splash* as a huge bucket of filthy water was flung over the mirror, completely covering the glass. Wolfie hurled the bucket at the glass as hard as he could, but it just bounced off.

'You fool!' yelled the reflection. 'You can't break a magic mirror! I am *indestructible*!' It tried to look towards Wolfie, but was just as filth-covered as the mirror and fumbled blindly about. 'Where are you?' it hissed, trying to wipe the mud from its face. 'I will find

you, don't you
worry about that!
And when I do,
I'll swap your
eyeballs for
Scotch eggs!
*Out-of-date
ones!'*

'Come on,
you two!' yelled
Wolfie to the
twins. 'We've got
to get out of here!'

'Thank goodness somebody sensible's
turned up!' said Gretel.

'*You'll regret this . . .*' ranted the mirror.

'Hey, Wolfie?' said Hansel as though
he hadn't heard anything the mirror

had said. 'Can you tell my sister that if she's trying to annoy me, she's doing a good job!'

'. . . I'll find out if you like Marmite or not! And if you *don't*, I'll bury you up to your neck in it . . .' continued the mirror.

'Oh, *really*!' said Gretel, ignoring the mirror's threats. 'Well, Wolfie, can you *please* inform my brother, that I couldn't give a—'

She stopped speaking as Wolfie grabbed them both by the hand and dragged them out of the room.

'Seriously! Once that mirror gets cleaned up, it is *not* going to be happy!' yelled Wolfie, 'We've got to go – *now*!'

———◆◆———

'*Come on!* Hurry up!' cried the reflection as a handful of imps struggled to wipe the mud off the mirror's surface. '*He'll* be here any minute, and I *still* look filthy.'

'*Who* will be here?' called a voice from a dark corner of the room.

'*Gah!*' shrieked the reflection, leaping high into the air and then trying to make it look as though it had just been doing some exercises. Out of the shadows stepped a magical projection of the troll Hurrilan, flickering in the dim light.

'Hurrilan! How *lovely* it is to see you!' the reflection exclaimed, shooing its imp underlings away. 'What an honour!'

'Be quiet,' said Hurrilan, and the reflection fell silent. 'The cutting. Is it growing? You've managed to use your master's magic?' The reflection nodded and Hurrilan looked pleased. 'That's good news,' said. 'When the Green Man refused to help me, I thought that was the end . . . but with *your* help, it seems we *will* have our own Story Tree – at last! *Everything* is going to plan!'

'Mmmm . . .' said the reflection.

'Sorry, what was that?'

'Yes, it's *almost* all going perfectly!'

'*Almost?* Is the cutting safe: yes or no?' asked Hurrilan.

'Yes-*ish?*' said the reflection in a small voice.

Hurrilan glared at him. 'Let's try this one more time . . . You have the cutting. It is growing, and everything is OK?'

'Yes, *but* . . .' began the reflection, then it noticed Hurrilan's expression and finished off with, 'but *actually*,

now I think about it . . . everything's *GREAT*!'

'Glad to hear it,' said the troll warlock, nodding. '*Please* make sure that you take *extremely* good care of that cutting. If *anything* were to happen to it, I would be *most* distressed.'

The mirror bobbed nervously. 'Yes – *yes*, of course!' it said.

Hurrilan narrowed his eyes. 'I sometimes do things I regret when I'm distressed,' he said. '*Awful* things . . . Do we understand each other?'

The reflection nodded, and gulped nervously as the image of Hurrilan vanished.

'Hey, Wolfie?' said Hansel. 'Can you ask my sister to walk downwind of me? It's *really* starting to smell round here.'

'Oh, Wolfie?' said Gretel. 'Guess what? I've invented a brand new word for *stupid* and you spell it like this: H-A-N-S-E-L.'

Hansel pretended to laugh. 'Oh that's *soooooo* funny, so *completely* hilarious! Wolfie? Can you *please* tell my—'

'*No!*' yelled Wolfie. Hansel and Gretel fell silent. Wolfie *tried* to glare at them like his dad, the Big Bad Wolf, glared at people, but the effect wasn't *quite* the same. His quivering little snout made him look confused, worried and upset. Gretel patted him on the shoulder.

'Sorry, Wolfie,' she said, 'I didn't

mean to upset you.'

'You two have *got* to sort this out!' said Wolfie. 'We're on a mission, *remember*?'

'Absolutely!' exclaimed Hansel. 'And we're *totally* going to succeed! Just as soon as we get rid of my dead-weight of a sister!'

'Oh, it's like *that*, is it?' yelled Gretel. 'Well, *fine*! Me and Wolfie were just leaving! Weren't we, Wolfie?'

'I don't *think* so!' snorted Hansel. 'Wolfie is coming with *me*! Right, Wolfie?'

Wolfie groaned. It was *exactly* the same with his dad and the people of Tale Town – he was *always* caught in the middle. Well, *no more*! Wolfie was going to put his foot down.

'No!' he said firmly. 'We are *not* splitting up! And stop arguing about who gets to keep me – I'm not your *pet*!' He stood there with his paws on his hips, his furry tail wagging behind him and his whiskers trembling. 'We're *all* going to have to find a way through this *together*! I mean, you know . . . so long as that's OK with you guys?'

7

Be Your Own Wolf

*T*he plan was to track the imps'
movements so they could work
out where the cutting was. *Then* the
plan was to take back the cutting and
sneak out without being seen. It was
Wolfie's plan and everyone agreed it
was a good one.

But it seemed that carrying out the
plan wasn't going to be that easy.
Gretel was silently tracking one of the

ZIPPPPP!

imps when Hansel fired a shot from his slingshot and tripped her up. The only reason that the imp didn't see her was because she happened to fall right into a pile of compost. Later, while Hansel had been climbing a rope to get to one of the higher l e v e l s of the p a l a c e, Gretel had fired a burning arrow that set fire to the rope and Hansel had to slide back down as quickly as he could.

'What?' Gretel had protested when Wolfie glared at her. 'It was an *accident!*'

Next, Wolfie had to stop Hansel trying to glue Gretel's hands to a door handle and Gretel chaining Hansel to a pillar.

'This is no good!' exploded Wolfie. 'We'll *never* find the cutting like this! You two are going to get us *all* captured!'

Then a thought occurred to him. It was quite a sneaky thought and it *almost* surprised him. He didn't normally 'do' sneaky, but perhaps there was more wolf in him than he realized.

'Hey, guys . . .' said Wolfie. 'Which one of you would be better at finding your way home? You know, if you were trapped in a forest and only had a handful of breadcrumbs or something?'

'That would be me,' began Hansel. 'Although I'd have to say that breadcrumbs are *not* an effective way of marking a route. What you *really* need are white pebbles, then—'

'What on earth are you going on about?' interrupted Gretel. 'Firstly, *I* am clearly the superior trail finder. Secondly the whole breadcrumbs thing was *your* idea, and thirdly—'

'Thirdly you smell?' interrupted Hansel.

'You are *so* immature!' yelled Gretel.

'At least I don't smell!' said Hansel.

While Hansel and Gretel were distracted, Wolfie crept silently away.

He hoped that the twins were going to be OK, but it was clear there was *no way* they would be able to work together right now. He was going to have to go it alone.

Everything was better now that Wolfie was free of the twins' constant arguing. He found that he could use his keen wolf nose to smell anyone that came near, and hide in plenty of time. All the imps he saw were going in one direction carrying fertilizer, water and plant food, then coming back carrying nothing but empty wooden buckets. They had to be going to the Story Tree cutting!

After a while, Wolfie was *almost* beginning to enjoy himself. He felt daring, brave, and like some sort of secret agent. He crept through the wooden corridors, silent as the night, pretending to be on an incredibly dangerous and important mission. Then he remembered that he *was* on a dangerous and important mission, and got all nervous again.

He took a few deep breaths to calm himself and carried on around the next corner.

'Hello,' said the man from the looking glass. 'Fancy seeing you here!'

'Eeeeaaarrrkkkk!' shrieked Wolfie, leaping backwards.

'Oh there's no need to worry!' said the reflection, as a couple of sweaty imps heaved the empty mirror along behind him on the wooden cart. 'After all, I can't *physically* harm you.'

Wolfie breathed a sigh of relief and

inched closer, trying to get past the reflection.

'However . . .' said the reflection, 'I do have . . . my UNDERLINGS!' He barked a command and another group of nervous imps stepped out of a door behind him.

'Come on, guys!' said Wolfie to the scared imps. 'I don't want to hurt anyone! Why don't you just let me past?'

The imps looked at each other, then Wolfie, then the reflection, and finally down at the floor as they shuffled their feet and moved out of the way. 'And you *really* shouldn't be working for him!' added Wolfie. 'He's *not at all* nice!'

'You're pathetic!' roared the reflection

at the imps. 'Looks like I'd better do this the old-fashioned way!' His eyes flashed with a sickly green light and the plants, branches and roots of the palace began to snake around, rearranging themselves into a new shape. A round sort of shape. A big, 'hole-y' kind of shape that was opening right beneath Wolfie's feet. He tried to step around it but the hole opened faster and faster. There was no way he could avoid it.

'Yeaaarrrrghhhhh!' yelled Wolfie as he lost his footing completely and tumbled into blackness.

8

The Instruction Manual

'**U**rrrnnnngh . . .' groaned Wolfie. He was sprawled out on a soft floor surrounded by straw, mouldy plants and the unmistakable smell of rot. Flies buzzed, worms slithered and unpleasant things crawled *everywhere*. Wolfie realized the awful truth: he was in a *massive compost heap*. 'Eeeeuuuchhh!' he squealed, leaping up and wiping off as much of the stinking mess as possible.

'*Ha!* Look at you now!' cackled the reflection from high above. 'Down with all the rubbish where you belong! I shall leave you down there until –' His voice cut off and Wolfie heard the reflection gasp. 'What? Hurrilan wants to speak to me *now*?'

There was a chattering reply from the imps, and

the reflection called down to Wolfie, 'Look, I've got some work to do, OK? I'll come back to carry on taunting you in a bit . . .'

'All right!' Wolfie yelled. 'No rush.'

'Thanks for being so understanding,' the reflection called back.

Then there was silence.

◆◆◆

Wolfie peered around in the gloom, hoping that he might find a way out. He explored every inch of the cavernous compost heap, but found nothing. The walls were so slick with rotting compost juice that each time he tried to climb up, he slid right back down, squelching into the filthy muck. Things were *not* looking good. 'Oh no you *don't!*' he

SNIFF!

muttered as he plucked a woodlouse from his ear. A worm was perched on the top of his hat, an earwig was trying to wriggle up his nose, and his best cravat was ruined. All in all, it wasn't the best day he'd ever had. So Wolfie did the only thing he could think of: he sat down on the floor and cried.

'Don't worry!' came a gentle voice. 'It's not *so* bad down here. Besides, there's plenty of food.'

'Who's there?' asked Wolfie, his heart pounding.

'Only me,' said a grubby-looking imp, poking his head out of the filth. 'I got banished for breaking the magic mirror's favourite mirror — he's very vain, you know. *"That's seven years' bad luck for you,"* the mirror said as he threw me down here, then he laughed.'

'That's *awful*!' said Wolfie.

'I know,' replied the imp. 'He makes some *really* lame jokes!'

'I was thinking more about being trapped down here for seven years.'

'Oh yeah, right. That too!'

'So what about the food you mentioned?' asked Wolfie. 'I am kind of hungry.'

The imp grinned as he rummaged

around in the filth and pulled out a juicy worm.

'Ohhh . . .' said Wolfie. 'You know what? I've just remembered – I'm not *actually* hungry *at all*! Isn't that odd?'

The imp shrugged and popped the worm into its mouth, chewing away happily as Wolfie tried not to be sick.

'So . . . what's your name?' asked the imp, its mouth full of half-chewed worm.

'Wolfie.'

'Hi, Wolfie, I'm Karpit.'

'Seriously? Like, the things you put on the floors?'

Karpit shrugged. 'Laugh all you like, but don't *ever* laugh at my uncle Dawmatte. He's got a black belt.'

'What in? Karate? Judo?'

'No, in his trousers!' said Karpit, looking confused. 'Still, we'd have to escape from *here* before you could start offending my uncle!' He slumped down on a pile of rotting dandelions, which slipped to one side, leaving him sprawled out on the filthy floor.

'Typical!' muttered Karpit.

'Wait!' exclaimed Wolfie. 'What's that . . . down where you were sitting? I can see something!'

Poking up out of the compost was the top of a book. Together they scrabbled in the dirt, digging away until Wolfie was able to pick it up and wipe it clean.

On the cover it had a picture of the magic looking glass, and the words:

iMirror
User's Guide

'Whoa!' exclaimed Karpit. 'What does it say?'

Wolfie opened the book and started reading. '"Congratulations on choosing iMirror. Most mirrors offer you a glimpse of the world around you;

iMirror gives you the world you want . . ."' He paused. 'It goes on like that for ages!' Wolfie skipped through a lot of pages. 'Wait! This sounds interesting, listen . . . "iMirror is manufactured to the highest standards, but if iMirror is left active for too long, it may develop personality 'issues'. If iMirror becomes 'problematic' you may switch it off, and return for a full refund, or simply break it using the enclosed magical hammer – bringing an end to any undesired magic. Please note your personal safety in either course of action is NOT guaranteed."' The magic mirror must have become faulty!' exclaimed Wolfie. Then his face fell. 'But without that hammer

we've got no chance of stopping it — we'd *never* get close enough to just turn it off!'

'Wait a minute!' cried Karpit. 'I saw something like that the other day!' He started scrabbling around, sending banana skins, carrot peelings and less recognizable, but equally disgusting things flying. 'Now where was it . . . ?' He dug on for a minute or two before holding a very dirty glass hammer in the air and shouting, 'A-ha!'

'Amazing!' exclaimed Wolfie. 'Now we've got everything we need, apart from a way out of here . . .'

There was a sharp chopping sound and wood chippings scattered down on top of them. A flare of light appeared about ten metres above their heads and a shadowy figure appeared.

'Oh no!' Wolfie cried. 'He's back! Quick, pass me the hammer – I'll hide it!'

Karpit shoved the hammer into Wolfie's hand and dived beneath the top layer of compost. The end of a rope slapped on to the ground. Wolfie managed to tuck the hammer under his shirt just as someone landed right in front of him.

'Hey, Wolfie!' said Gretel. 'Nice place you've got here!'

9

A Comedy of Errors

Gretel shimmied back up the rope and heaved Wolfie through the hole she had hacked, but the branches were already weaving together. Wolfie only just managed to drag Karpit through, too, before the hole closed completely.

'I know how to do it!' gasped Wolfie, as they crouched behind some ferns in one of the living palace's long corridors.

'Do what?' asked Gretel.

'Fix *everything*!' replied Wolfie. He held up the hammer that Karpit had found. 'We can destroy the magic mirror and get you and Hansel back to normal!'

Gretel growled at Hansel's name.

'Whatever!' exclaimed Wolfie. 'What we need to do *now* is get to the cutting. I *bet* the mirror won't be too far away!'

Gretel smiled. 'I know where the cutting is! I was following some imps up to the main tower when I heard the mirror drop you into that compost heap. So all we have to do is fight our way to the top of the tower – despite the *very* real chance of almost certain death – find the cutting, and escape through a courtyard full of trolls.'

'Now you put it like that . . .' began Wolfie.

'I'm in!' cried Gretel.

'And me!' squeaked a trembling Karpit.

'Right then.' Wolfie gulped, his whiskers trembling in terror. 'Let's go.'

Wolfie, Gretel and Karpit soon arrived at the foot of a huge spiral staircase that twisted around the edge of a tall circular tower. They could see all the way to the top, hundreds of metres above.

'This is the main tower,' whispered Gretel. She pointed at a group of imps parading around in mismatched and ill-fitting armour on the third floor. 'But we're going to have to get past without *them* seeing us.'

'How?' asked Karpit.

'Using *this*!' replied Gretel, swinging a grappling hook on a rope through the air and throwing it a few levels above the imps, to catch over a twisting handrail. 'Quick, while they're not looking!'

Wolfie and Karpit clambered on to the rope behind her.

Unfortunately, it turned out that Wolfie and Karpit were *not* good at rope climbing.

'My hands hurt!' complained Karpit.

'Hurry up!' whispered Gretel.

'*You* try climbing a rope with *paws*!' muttered Wolfie. 'You have no idea how hard this is without thumbs!'

'Shhh!' hissed Gretel.

A surprised-looking imp peered over

the handrail. With a nasty grin, it pulled out a jagged dagger and started sawing away at the rope.

Gretel groaned and hooked her candy-cane staff into the wall. 'Grab my legs!' she yelled as the last threads of the rope gave way, leaving Karpit clinging on to Wolfie's back while he dangled from Gretel's feet.

'*This* isn't easy with paws *either*!' yelped Wolfie.

'Hang on!' shouted Gretel, rocking her body back and forth until Wolfie was swinging over the staircase.

'Let go on the next swing!' grunted Gretel through gritted teeth.

'I'm not sure . . .' began Wolfie, but Gretel kicked her legs so hard that his paws slipped and he and Karpit landed in a heap on the stairs. Gretel took one more swing, then flung herself over the handrail, landing in a crouch, before springing up to climb the stairs two at a time.

As Wolfie got to his feet, he noticed a figure a couple of floors above – it was Hansel! If Hansel and Gretel found each other then it was game over! He *had* to keep them apart! But how?

Wolfie didn't deal well with stress. It was like those granny-eating lessons at Wolf School where he *knew* the answers but as soon as he was actually *asked*, his mind went blank and he couldn't remember whether you were meant eat the granny *first* and *then* disguise yourself as an old lady, or the other way around.

A great roar rose up below him and Wolfie looked down to see trolls pouring into the tower and start running towards the stairs. Wolfie's mind raced, and *then* he had an idea . . .

'*Trolls!*' shouted Wolfie, pointing to the base of the tower.

'I'm on it!' yelled Gretel, skidding through the badly dressed imps on the third floor, who all scattered, whimpering about it not being their fault. Gretel picked up a big axe one of the imps had dropped and started running back downstairs towards the trolls.

'Let's go!' yelled Wolfie to Karpit as they raced past Gretel up the stairs.

'*Wolfie!*' cried Hansel, as Wolfie finally made it to the sixth floor. His eyes narrowed as he saw Karpit and he pulled out his nunchucks.

'It's OK!' yelped Wolfie. 'He's with me! We've got to get to the top of the tower – that's where the cutting is. Come on!' Hansel looked puzzled, but shrugged, and together they all ran up the staircase.

'Oh yeah, watch out for the cuddlers!' called Hansel as they raced along a narrow section of the staircase lined with big, bushy plants that had incredibly soft leaves and made a purring sound.

'Cuddlers?' asked Wolfie. Hansel poked his candy-cane staff at one of the plants. Two big bushy arms shot out and tightly cuddled the candy cane. The purring got even louder.

'They're not really dangerous,' explained Hansel, 'but it took me *ages* to get free after one of them got hold of me!'

As they ran on, Wolfie peered down to see Gretel hacking through the staircase with the axe. With a sudden crash, the bottom two floors, *and* the trolls, fell back down to the bottom of the tower.

'At least we're a good way above,' thought Wolfie. 'It'll take her ages to catch up!'

Just then Gretel fired an arrow with a rope on it towards the floor they were on and started swiftly climbing up.

'Gahh!' muttered Wolfie.

'What's down there?' asked Hansel, frowning.

'Nothing!' lied Wolfie, while he tried to work out what to do. 'Actually, it's *trolls*!' he said, surprised at how easy he was finding it to fib. 'Hundreds of them! We've got to hide!' He shoved Hansel into a hollow tree trunk and whispered, *'Stay out of sight!'*

Wolfie's heart raced. Gretel was nearly up to their level . . . What now? He spotted a couple of cuddlers right next to where she was going to climb over the handrail. He knew that he *should* warn her, but then the twins would definitely see each other again – and *then* what? He kept quiet and stood just out of sight.

As soon as Gretel heaved herself over the railing, the cuddler scooped her up into a huge, warm hug that completely surrounded her.

'The trolls have gone!' Wolfie whispered to Hansel a moment later. 'Let's go!' He grinned as they ran up the last few steps. They were so close! It looked like everything was going to be all right! He'd *never* felt better.

Suddenly a swarm of imps poured out of the door at the top of the staircase and came running towards them, roaring and waving a ragtag collection of weapons. The weapons were mostly held backwards or upside down, but they were *still* weapons.

To make things even worse, Gretel came running up the stairs and spotted Hansel.

'*This ends NOW!*' she yelled, pulling out her bow and sending arrow after arrow whistling through the air. Hansel ducked as the arrows flew overhead and thunked into the wall. The imps stopped where they were, looking nervous. For a moment nobody did anything, then something strange happened to Wolfie. He *knew* what to do, and he *actually* felt as though he could do it. Time seemed to slow down as he watched Hansel and Gretel approach each other, their faces twisted in anger. Wolfie felt strangely calm. He *had* to rescue the cutting; he *had* to destroy the mirror. Nothing else mattered.

He climbed up the arrows that were stuck into the wall as though they were rungs on a ladder. Then he leaped into the air, caught hold of a vine and swung over the heads of the confused imps. He let go of the vine at full swing and flew through the open door into the room where the cutting was.

He sprang up immediately, his senses alert and tingling. *There* was the cutting from the Story Tree, floating in the air, suspended in a stream of powerful magic. Wolfie didn't stop to think. He reached out to grab it — but as he did so, everything else faded into darkness. It was only then that he noticed the man from the magic looking glass in the shadows on the far side of the room, smiling horribly.

It had all been a trap.

10

Through the Looking Glass

*W*olfie found himself alone in a strangely blank space. It was neither dark nor light, just empty. It was hard to tell if he was standing on something or floating in the air.

'Where am I?' asked Wolfie, but everything sounded strange, as though he was underwater.

'I suppose you're wondering where your precious cutting is?' echoed the voice of the magic looking glass, though he was nowhere to be seen. 'What you saw in that room was just a reflection, a copy. The *real* cutting is hidden here – in a world of my own creation – beyond *anything* you could imagine.'

'Oh, I don't know . . .' replied Wolfie. 'I've got a pretty good imagination. Do you have any greybows?'

'Greybows?'

'Yeah, you know. Like a rainbow that's just grey, not different colours.'

'Er . . . well, no. But I *could* make some. I *easily* could!'

'What about spider shoes?'

'You mean shoes for a spider?'

'No!' laughed Wolfie. 'I mean shoes that have spider legs and can walk around by themselves. Pretty cool, right?'

'*No!*' came the mirror's voice. '*Not* cool. I'm not talking about any of that, I'm talking about a world of *terror*! A world of *dread* . . .'

Wolfie nodded. 'Sorry . . . I talk too much when I'm nervous, or worried, or scared, and I just—'

The mirror interrupted him, sounding

cross, 'You're doing it again!'

'Sorry . . .'

'*Anyway* . . .' said the mirror loudly. 'How about I offer you a chance to escape?' Wolfie nodded eagerly. 'So it's agreed!' the mirror continued. 'If you manage to overcome your worst fears, you may go free and take the stupid tree cutting with you. And if you don't . . . then you will be trapped here – *forever*!'

Trees shot up out of the nothingness and smoke poured into the blank space, creating a dark sky. Seconds later Wolfie was standing trembling in a small clearing, as the mirror's echoing laugh faded away in the cool night air.

Wolfie glanced round, his heart racing. The reflection had said he would be trapped within a world of his worst fears, and Wolfie had many, *many* fears . . .

While he waited to be attacked by an army of giant zombie beetles with laser eyes and swords for legs, Wolfie noticed a movement in the bushes near to him. He was surprised to see a little old lady hurrying along with a small basket over one arm. She didn't look *particularly* frightening . . . although one old lady had got *really* angry when he accidentally splashed mud on her dress, so you never could tell.

Another bush rustled, and in the darkness he saw his father, the Big Bad Wolf, creeping along behind the old lady. Wolfie's heart sank, he knew *exactly* how this was going to end! Then Wolfie saw something that gave him hope. There *he* was in the bushes too – *another* Wolfie, though it looked like a different version of him. *This* Wolfie looked as though he needed a good bath and hadn't ironed his clothes in *FOREVER*! Still, as long as the scruffy Wolfie could get to the old lady before his dad, then *hopefully* she'd be able to get away.

Wolfie watched as Scruffy Wolfie crept up towards the old lady and tapped her on the arm.

'Do you need some help?' he said kindly. The old lady nodded. 'You should be careful in these woods,' said Scruffy Wolfie. '*Terrible* things can happen.'

'Oh, I know!' replied the old lady. 'I got lost, you see. Thank you for offering to help!'

'Think nothing of it!' replied Scruffy

Wolfie. 'It's my pleasure!' Something about the way he said this made Wolfie's nerves jangle, and the next second . . . Scruffy Wolfie leaped forward and gobbled the old lady up in one bite.

'NOooOOoOooOooooO!' shrieked Wolfie.

Scruffy Wolfie turned to face him and grinned horribly. '*This* is your greatest fear,' he said. 'You're a *wolf*! Deep down you know that it's true – you can't fight it forever.'

Wolfie's heart pounded as the woodland scene melted away into nothing.

———◆◆———

For a while everything went dark again, then large oak trees sprouted up and Wolfie found himself in a sun-dappled forest next to a path lined with pretty wild flowers. He frowned: *this* didn't seem very scary. Then he heard the sound of a girl singing softly to herself as she skipped along the path. There was a rustling in the bushes next to him and his stomach churned as he saw a grey wolf-tail darting forward like a shark's fin.

'Look out!' yelled Wolfie to the girl. '*Run!*'

But the girl didn't seem to hear him.

Scruffy Wolfie emerged from the bushes and smiled at the girl as he leaned against a tree. 'Your grandmother is ill in bed and has been asking for you,' he said with a wicked grin. 'Do hurry straight there!'

'Don't listen!' shouted Wolfie. '*It's a trap!*'

But it was no good. The girl thanked Scruffy Wolfie and ran off deep into the forest. Then the whole scene drifted away as though the trees were made of mist.

Moments later, Wolfie watched as an old wooden cottage built itself in the blankness next to him. Tall trees shot up around the edge of a small picket fence and, finally, a brightly painted door swung shut and the scene was complete. He crept forward and peered in through the window to see Scruffy Wolfie lying in bed wearing a really, *really* unconvincing granny disguise.

'Seriously?' thought Wolfie. 'That disguise is *terrible*! It's *totally* obvious that it's a wolf!'

His thoughts were interrupted by a knock at the door. It was the girl. Wolfie ran over and tried to block her path, but she just walked straight through him as though he wasn't even there.

'Wolves are wolves,' sneered his father, appearing from nowhere behind Wolfie. 'That's all there is to it! And *you* are a wolf.'

'No!' shouted Wolfie. 'I won't let this happen!'

'Too late,' said the Big Bad Wolf. 'It's happening *right now* . . .'

———◆◆———

The scene shifted again and now Wolfie was inside the house, right next to the bed where Scruffy Wolfie lay, pretending to be the girl's grandmother.

'My! What big slippers you have, Grandmother!' said the girl looking around the room at the scattered possessions.

'All the better to . . . er . . . keep my feet warm with?' said Scruffy Wolfie, then shook his head and roared. 'Oh, who cares about all that rubbish! I'm *hungry*!'

He leaped out of bed, ripping off his granny disguise – a nightmare vision of claws and fangs. The girl jumped back, screaming, and for a moment Wolfie was paralysed with fear. Everything seemed to move in slow motion as he watched the scruffy version of himself leap towards the terrified girl.

'No . . .' he whimpered, feeling disgusted by how pathetic he sounded.

'*No!*' he repeated more

forcefully, anger rising up inside him.

'*NO!*' he yelled as he sprang towards the evil Wolfie.

His mind raced – it didn't *have* to be this way. He could be whoever he *wanted* to be. It doesn't matter what his father thought, or how the people of Tale Town felt about wolves. *He* didn't need to be on *either* side: he just needed to be himself.

'I would *never* do that!' he yelled, and then howled his loudest, most wolfish *HOWL* at the evil Wolfie and the Big Bad Wolf. They both tumbled backwards into nothing as the bedroom dissolved around him. This time the girl *did* see him. She smiled gratefully and then she too disappeared.

Seconds later Wolfie was back in the nowhere place with the cutting from the Story Tree floating in front of him.

'No!' screamed the magic looking glass. 'I don't understand! You should have been trapped *forever*! You should still be whimpering and screaming something like "*Help, noooo! The giant ants are drinking my brains with a curly straw!*" What went wrong? What did you see? What was your greatest fear?'

Wolfie grinned. 'That *I* might be as bad as *you* are! But *nobody's* going to make me do *anything* that I don't want to!' He reached out and grabbed the cutting. 'So if you don't mind, I think *I'll* be taking this!'

11

The Dilemma

$\mathcal{A}$s soon as Wolfie grabbed the cutting, he was transported back through the mirror's glassy surface and into the Green Man's palace. He looked around in confusion. Instead of being at the top of the tower, he was in the centre of a large hall which was *filled* with terrifying statues like the ones in the courtyard. Hideous, ferocious animals and wild-looking men and women surrounded Wolfie, their faces twisted in snarling rage. He watched as a sea of imps poured in from the doorway that led out to the tower.

Seconds later the reflection burst out of the mirror and lunged towards Wolfie, passing straight through him.

'I can't believe that *you*, a pathetic, feeble excuse for a wolf, could have beaten *my* magical trap!' roared the reflection. Wolfie shrugged and was about to reply when he was distracted by a loud yell. He turned to see Hansel and Gretel burst into the room, still fighting bitterly. Behind them was a crowd of confused-looking trolls.

'*Stop it!*' yelled Wolfie. 'I've got the cutting! We can get out of here!'

'Great work, Wolfie!' shouted Hansel. 'Just let me finish this off . . .'

'I don't *think* so!' yelled Gretel, swinging a huge branch at Hansel, who only just ducked in time. 'Hang on! I won't be a minute, Wolfie!'

'Make them *stop!*' commanded Wolfie turning to face the reflection. 'Put things back to normal.'

'Or *what*?' asked the reflection.

'Or . . . *this*!' replied Wolfie, pulling out the glass hammer from under his shirt and waving it in the air. 'Either you break the spell on them, or I break you *and* your magic!'

Wolfie wasn't sure what he'd been expecting. He'd never really done much negotiating before – unless it was to negotiate with one of his brothers by squealing, '*Please stop twisting my arm, it's really starting to hurt!*' Even so, he

136

hadn't expected the reflection to laugh.

'Didn't you hear me?' added Wolfie. 'This hammer will *destroy* you!'

'Yes, *yes*, I know!' chuckled the reflection. 'I saw that you had it earlier. Why do you think I had the imps move the mirror to this hall?'

Wolfie frowned. 'For a change of scenery?'

'Look around,' said the reflection. 'You see all these statues? You see how *wild* and *frightening* they look?'

Wolfie nodded.

'Well, all these statues will come *back to life* if you use that hammer. It was *me* that turned them into statues in the first place! Without my magic, you'll be at their mercy!' Again the mirror laughed. 'So how about you give me back that cutting, and I'll *think* about letting you and your friends leave in one piece. Deal?'

Wolfie looked at the terrifying beasts. There was one in particular that looked incredibly scary. It was a man with a beard made of thorny brambles that snaked through the air, the razor-sharp thorns glinting in the light. It was clear that he'd never survive if they were all freed. Perhaps if he made a run for it now, he could get out of here with the cutting . . . but what about Hansel and Gretel? They'd be enemies for the rest of their lives, and it would be *his* fault. But if he returned the cutting, there was no

guarantee that the mirror man would keep his word.

Wolfie took a deep breath, and did the only thing that he could. He hurled the cutting at Hansel and Gretel. 'Catch!' he yelled as he dived towards the looking glass and swung the glass hammer forward as hard as he could.

12

The Awakening

*T*iny shards of multicoloured glass spun through the air as the magic looking glass shattered. Glittering splinters scattered across the floor, along with a pair of shiny silver shears, which Wolfie lunged towards and grabbed. For a moment the reflection stood in the middle of the hall, looking shocked, angry and scared, then it too broke into millions of pieces, which blew away on a howling wind.

Wolfie braced himself as the entire hall shook with the power of the released magic. There was a sound like a frozen lake thawing, a rushing creak that became a roar. First one, then another of the statues eased back into life, and seconds later Wolfie stood in the middle of a seething mass of furious wild animals and monsters. He tried to bravely accept his fate – but

Wolfie was *terrified*. The last thing he saw was Hansel and Gretel's panicked faces as the army of creatures closed in around him.

'*Stop!*' rang out a voice with a deep woody echo. '*All of you!*' Wolfie peered out through one half-closed eye as the creatures fell silent. 'We have been rescued! The looking glass is gone!' continued the tall figure with the thorny beard as he knelt down by Wolfie. 'And I believe it is *this* brave young wolf who has saved us!' As he spoke, the brambles and thorns in his beard died away and were replaced with brightly coloured flowers and ivy.

'So you're not going to do anything horrible to me?' asked Wolfie.

The tall man with the floral hair and beard smiled. 'Not at all! When I discovered that my magic looking glass had betrayed me, my friends and I tried to fight back, but the mirror cast a spell, turning us all into statues. I should imagine that we looked quite fearsome!'

'Kind of . . .' replied Wolfie, opening both eyes fully.

There was a sudden scuffle as Karpit ran over, wielding a rusty sword and waggling it around under the noses of the various animals and people. 'You leave my friend alone!' the tiny imp yelled as loudly as he could.

The Green Man laughed kindly. 'You're a very brave young imp! But don't worry, we're all safe now. The magic looking glass has been destroyed.'

'And so has all of –'

'– its magic!' exclaimed Hansel and Gretel as they ran over, safely carrying the cutting from the Story Tree.

'Well done, Wolfie, you –'

'– *totally* saved the day!'

'Only one more thing to do!' said the Green Man. 'We have some uninvited guests who have outstayed their welcome.' He pointed through the doorway at a group of worried-looking

trolls who were sneaking away. 'I think it's time that our "friends" left, don't you?'

The assorted pack of wild animals roared in agreement and raced out of the room to help drive away the trolls.

'And you can tell Hurrilan,' the Green Man bellowed out of the window at the scattering army, 'that my magic is *not* his to use!'

Then he turned back to the rest of the imps, who were looking nervously at each other and slowly backing out of the hall. 'Well, this place is going to need a lot of tidying!' He smiled at Karpit. 'Do you and your friends want to help? I'll pay you all the worms you can eat!'

With a relieved cheer the imps set

to work. Karpit waved cheerfully over at Wolfie as he found a particularly fat, juicy worm and gobbled it up like spaghetti.

13

The Truth Will Out

*T*he journey back to Tale Town didn't take long, but then again, when you're sitting in the branches of a walking tree that can step over rivers in one stride it doesn't take long to get *anywhere.*

'Can you really can get *any* tree to do this?' Wolfie asked the Green Man.

'Pretty much,' replied the Green Man. 'You just have to ask nicely.

Wait a minute – I think someone down there is trying to get our attention . . .'

He peered down at a man on the ground who was waving a sword at them and shouting, 'You can't leave your tree here! Besides, all strangers have to be assessed by *His Worthiness* before entering Tale Town.'

'But we live here!' yelled Hansel and Gretel. 'And who's "*His Worthiness*"?'

'The mayor, of course!' replied the guard. 'But he's very busy, so you'll have to make an appointment.'

'Trust me,' said Gretel, holding up the Sacred Shiny Story-Snipping Shears. 'He'll want to see *us* right away.'

———◆◆———

It wasn't long before Wolfie, the twins and the Green Man were waiting in the mayor's office.

The guard instructed them to sit quietly, not touch anything, and to basically pretend that they weren't there, then left the room.

'What do you think of that creepy picture?' asked Hansel, pointing at a painting of someone who must have been Mayor Fitch's great-great-great-great-great-grandfather.

'Nice wig,' said Gretel. 'I might get one like that!' She stood in front of the painting so it looked like the curly white wig was perched on her own head. Hansel laughed as he playfully shoved Gretel out of the way so he could have a turn, but as he did, she fell against the picture frame, which tilted to one side. Suddenly there was a deep rumbling as a bookcase behind them swung open like a door.

Hansel and Gretel looked guiltily at each other. Wolfie's eyes widened and the Green Man shook his head with a smile.

'*Whoops!*' muttered Gretel as she peered through the doorway. It led into a dusty cupboard that was empty, apart from a large stone with text carved into it.

'Hey, look!' she whispered. 'This is

where Mayor Fitch keeps the "Live Long the Story Tree" poem.'

'Wait a minute . . .' said Hansel. They all peered closely at the stone, and Gretel gasped.

'The poem's different!' she cried. 'The poem we know goes like this:

"Long ago, upon this spot the Story
    Tree was born,
And with it grew up Tale Town, a
    rose without a thorn.

"Beware the shadows lurking in the
    darkness of the night,
Who want to take away this gift and
    hide from us its light.

"For if this tree is damaged then
    expect the unexpected,
The Story Tree is sacred and must
    always be protected.

"Live long the Story Tree!"

'But listen to what it says on *this* stone – it's the rest of the poem!

"Live long the Story Tree! A tree that's like no other,
A tree that could repair the world, turn enemies to brothers.

"Grow strong the Story Tree! A tree for all things living,
For stories should be freely shared, the gift is in the giving."'

For a moment everyone was silent.

'That changes the poem *completely*!' Hansel cried. '*Someone* must have broken the stone in half. The Story Tree is meant to be shared with everyone –

and Mayor Fitch knows it! He's been keeping this a secret!'

They were distracted by the sound of footsteps in the hallway. They rushed back to their seats and Hansel tilted the picture straight again. The book case rumbled shut just as the doorway opened and the mayor walked in. 'What was that noise?' he asked.

'That was me – *sorry*!' said the Green Man, wafting his hand back and forth in the air.

'I see . . .' said Mayor Fitch, his nose crinkling in disgust. Then he remembered what he was doing and put on his biggest, most charming smile. 'I hear that you have news about our Sacred Shiny Story-Snipping Shears?'

'Not just news!' replied Hansel with a grin, as Gretel pulled the shears out and handed them to the mayor.

'Well done!' enthused Mayor Fitch, his eyes lighting up greedily. 'You have done Tale Town a great service. The names Handel, Greta and Wolfo will be remembered as heroes!'

'Those aren't our names . . .' said Wolfie, but the mayor just smiled and continued:

'What a treat to see such a well-trained wolf! One who seeks to *help* humans – to *serve* them. It is indeed a proud day!'

'Well, I wasn't exactly *serving* . . .' said Wolfie, but again the mayor ignored him.

'Did you manage to reclaim the cutting that the trolls stole, too?' he asked, his eyes flashing keenly.

'I'm afraid not,' said the Green Man, giving a secret wink to Hansel, Gretel and Wolfie. 'The trolls were unable to use my magic properly and the cutting withered and died.'

'Oh that *is* a shame . . .' said the mayor, looking as regretful as he could. 'Still, at least it's not in the hands of the trolls, eh? After all, the poem does say that the Story Tree *must* be protected!'

'Yes,' agreed Hansel and Gretel. 'We *all* know the poem.'

'Anyway, I'm sure you have lots of *very* important things to do . . .' said the mayor. 'You now have my permission to enter Tale Town.' He shook hands with the Green Man and Wolfie, then wiped his hand on his trousers when he thought no one was looking.

'Thanks again!' he called, his smile falling from his face as soon as they had left the room. 'My guards will escort you out!'

As they left the Town Hall, Hansel turned to the Green Man. 'That was quick thinking to lie about the cutting!' he whispered.

'Well, I'm not entirely sure that your friend Mr Fitch can be trusted,' replied the Green Man. 'I think perhaps it's a good idea for *you* to keep the cutting safe for now.'

14

The Secret Garden

Although Tale Town was still on troll alert, Mayor Fitch had finally found someone to blame for breaking the Moonstone defences. Apparently it had been someone's Fairy Godmother (or Godbrother, or Godsister, or Godniece) and the mayor and his guards were busy tracking down as many fairies as they could to try to work out exactly who was responsible.

People were once again allowed to move around Tale Town as they pleased, so Hansel and Gretel called for a TOP SECRET meeting with their friends later that day.

'What's going on?' asked Anansi as soon as he saw the twins, his eyes bright with excitement.

'I'm so glad you're OK!' cried Red.

'What happened?' asked Jack.

'Whaaat!?' squawked Betsy.

'Sorry, Betsy!' laughed Gretel. 'We didn't get you a present, but we *have* got an *incredible* story to tell.'

'But we need to go somewhere *really* private first . . .' said Hansel. 'Come on, let's go to the beach.'

Between them, the twins, Wolfie and the Green Man explained the whole amazing story. Anansi clapped Wolfie on the back when he heard how Wolfie had risked his life to save the twins. Jack and Red gasped when they explained about the secret second half to the Story Tree poem, and *everybody* had been astonished to see a tiny silver shoot sprout out of the cutting that held *all* the details of their recent adventure.

The only person who hadn't really

warmed to Wolfie was Betsy. She kept looking sideways at him with her beady little eyes and muttering 'Whaaaaaat...' under her breath.

'What's up, Betsy?' asked Red and jumped as Betsy clucked a *very* loud, *very* threatening 'WHAaAaaaAaaat?'.

'Oh, *come on*, Betsy!' Jack said with a laugh. 'So what if he's the Big Bad Wolf's son? That whole business with Red's nan was probably just a big misunderstanding – right, Wolfie?'

'Um . . .' Wolfie blushed. 'Well, not exactly . . .' He noticed that Red was looking a bit nervous. 'But that's my *dad*,' he added firmly. 'I'm *me*! And I can *promise* you that I'd never do *anything* like that. Besides,' he added pulling out a little bag of nuts, 'I'm a vegetarian. So what are we going to do with this tree cutting then?'

'I've got an idea . . .' said Red, looking relieved. 'How about we pay our Sea Witch friend Lily a visit?'

———◆◆———

'I'm *sooooo* hyped to see you guys!' exclaimed Lily as she flicked her fish-tail to swim around her cave, deep under the sea. Wolfie was looking around in wonder as a school of fish drifted past him. It was Lily's magic that had brought them all down under the sea and *somehow* that same magic meant that you didn't do anything horrible like drown, either – though as Lily was only an apprentice Sea Witch, her magic didn't last for very long.

'So . . . what can I do you for?' asked Lily. 'You need to buy some spells?' Her luminous eyes shone even brighter.

'Not today, thanks,' explained Jack. 'We need to ask you a favour, actually . . .'

Lily's face flickered through a hundred different expressions as they told her about the cutting from the Story Tree and why they needed to hide it.

'Sure, I mean you can definitely *try* to grow it down here,' said Lily, 'though I'm not very green-fingered . . .' She looked at her green-tinted webbed fingers and sighed. 'You know what I mean? I'm not very good with plants!'

'It doesn't matter!' explained the Green Man. 'I can put a spell on the cutting so that it will grow here, regardless of what you do to it! Besides, it's not like you can forget to water it!'

Together, Lily and the Green Man cast a spell to transport a small section of the woods from just outside Red's garden down into Lily's cave in a huge bubble, which he placed in the middle of a bright beam of sunlight.

'That should do nicely!' he said as he planted the cutting inside the bubble. 'I'll check in every now and then,' he added, 'but you shouldn't have any problems.'

'*Awesome!*' exclaimed Lily breathlessly. 'An underwater tree! I've always wanted to try climbing a tree! And riding a bike! *And* trampolining. Any of you guys got an old trampoline you don't want?' Everybody shook their heads. 'Well, you'd better head home now! My magic's about to run out and then it would be "drowny-wowny" time!' She laughed brightly and waved goodbye as the whirlpool that had brought them down to her cave carried them all back up to the surface.

'See you soon!' she called out through the rushing bubbles. '*Adiós! Au revoir! Auf Wiedersehen* . . .'

And that was it. It was done: the cutting from the Story Tree was safe. Wolfie and the Green Man were taken to see *all* the amazing things that Tale Town had to offer – including Greentop's Cafe, where you could eat happiness-flavoured toast; the market stall where you could buy a (temporary) flying potion; and the brand-new X-TREME petting zoo, with its baby dragons, griffins and a phoenix.

Wolfie looked round at his new friends and smiled. He'd never *really* felt like he fitted in anywhere. But now – for the first time ever – he felt like he'd come home.

The End

Hansel

Strengths: Climbing, jumping, sneaking and pouncing – basically anything ninja-like

Weaknesses: Playing the violin

Likes: His twin sister, Gretel, nunchucks and gingerbread

Dislikes: Broccoli, and any other vegetable that looks like a miniature tree

Wolfie

Strengths: Empathy, understanding, caring and thoughtfulness

Weaknesses: Well, for a wolf, most of the things listed above aren't super-useful

Likes: Blow-drying his hair and coconut shampoo

Dislikes: Being mean, rude or aggressive – can't we all just get along?

Gretel

Strengths: Running, leaping, springing and balancing – basically, anything ninja-like

Weaknesses: Playing the tuba

Likes: Her twin brother, Hansel, candy-cane weapons and gingerbread

Dislikes: Evil magic mirrors and being bored

Hurrilan

Strengths: ALL types of troll magic and a commanding presence

Weaknesses: His anger often clouds his judgement

Likes: Smokey Goat-flavoured crisps

Dislikes: The way Tale Town people keep the Story Tree to themselves